TIM AND GINGER

by

Edward Ardizzone

OXFORD UNIVERSITY PRESS
Oxford New York Toronto Melbourne

Oxford University Press, Walton Street, Oxford OX2 6DP

OXFORD NEW YORK TORONTO
DELHI BOMBAY CALCUTTA MADRAS KARACHI
PETALING JAYA SINGAPORE HONG KONG TOKYO
NAIROBI DAR ES SALAAM CAPE TOWN
MELBOURNE AUCKLAND

and associated companies in
BEIRUT BERLIN IBADAN NICOSIA

Oxford is a trade mark of Oxford University Press

ISBN *0 19 279614 3 (HARDCOVER)*
0 19 272113 5 (SOFTCOVER)

First published 1965
Reprinted 1970, 1973, 1980, 1987

To my grandchildren, Daniel and Hannah.

Printed in Hong Kong

Tim was a small boy who lived in a house by the sea.

Every day, when the weather was fine, he and his best friend, Ginger, would play on the beach.

When the tide was high and the sea came right up to the steep shingle bank, Tim and Ginger would play ducks and drakes by throwing flat pebbles so they skipped across the water.

Ginger was very good at this.

When the tide was low and the sea went far out, they would dig in the sand for lug worms which they sold to the fishermen for bait.

Tim, because he worked harder, always found more worms than Ginger.

However, what Tim liked to do best was to sit and talk with the old boatman who would tell him all about the sea and ships.

This sometimes bored Ginger, who thought he knew everything about everything, though of course he did not. ‘Poof!’ he would say. ‘I have been a sailor boy and know all about the silly old sea.’ Then he would go off and practise playing ducks and drakes and get even better at it than before.

One day, they found the old boatman looking sad and serious.

'Ah!' he said. 'Have you heard about poor Tom, the baker's son? Went shrimping he did among the rocks under the high chalk cliffs and was caught by the tide. He will never come home no more.'

Then he went on to say that tides were dangerous and that, if they would stop and listen, he would tell them why.

Tim stayed to listen, but Ginger only said, 'Poof! I know all about the silly old tides,' and went off to play ducks and drakes again.

The next day the sea was so calm and blue that it did not look at all dangerous.

Ginger wanted Tim to play with him but Tim had to go into the town with his parents.

'O.K.!' said Ginger. 'I will see you at tea-time. Now I am going shrimping.'

Tim begged Ginger to be careful.

'Poof!' answered Ginger. 'I am not afraid of your silly old tides.'

When Tim arrived back he hurried to the beach. It was tea-time and there was nobody about. He looked everywhere for Ginger but could not find him. Worse still, the tide was coming in.

Tim was worried. He felt sure that Ginger was somewhere under those tall white cliffs and could not get back. He wondered what to do, when he noticed a little boat just afloat on the incoming tide.

At once, Tim made up his mind. He would take the boat and go to the rescue.

He waded through the shallow water to the boat, climbed on board, pulled in the

anchor, unshipped the oars and rowed away to the tall white cliffs which he could just see in the far distance.

It was a long, long row and Tim was

tired, but he kept grimly on.

He was desperately worried, because, now that he was getting near the cliffs, he could see that the rocks at their base had been covered by the rising tide, and he knew that

Ginger could not swim. And nowhere could he see any sign of Ginger.

He had almost given up hope of ever seeing him again, when rounding a bend of the cliff, he saw something red just above the water.

It was Ginger. He was in a terrible plight. By standing on the tips of his toes, he could only just keep his head above the sea.

However, he was soon on board and seemed none the worse for his adventure.

Tim was tired after his long row, so he

let Ginger take the oars and row them home.

Now Ginger was an excitable boy. While he rowed he became more and more excited, telling Tim about his adventures. How the crabs nibbled his toes and how a sea-gull sat on his head, and when he came to how a great shark swam very close, he was so excited that he let the oars drop in the water and drift away.

Tim was horrified. He knew that now they were at the mercy of the wind and waves.

And indeed they were. The wind began to blow, the waves to rise, and the boat to drift towards some unknown shore.

Tim stood up in the boat and waved his

red jersey, but nobody saw them. Soon it became dark so, cold and wet and miserable, they curled themselves up in the bottom of the boat and tried to go to sleep.

By this time it was blowing a gale.

Now when Tim and Ginger did not get home for supper all sorts of things started to happen.

First of all the man who owned the boat was angry.

'That boy Tim has stolen my boat,' he said. 'Arrest him and put him in prison.'

'Nonsense,' said the old boatman. 'Tim is too honest a boy to steal anything. He must have taken it for a good reason.'

All the same the old boatman was anxious. He kept looking through his telescope in the hope of seeing the boys. He wished they were back as he did not like the look of the weather.

Tim's mother was worried. His father said, 'It is all right, my dear. Tim is a sensible boy, he will come to no harm.' Though, of course, he was worried too.

But when night fell and a gale was blowing and the great waves were crashing on the beach, all were very frightened for the safety of the boys.

The alarm was given. Parties of men and women armed with torches were sent to search the rocky shores and pebbly beaches. The coast-guards were warned, and all

along the cliff tops were watchers. Guards with their telescopes, old gentlemen with their binoculars and children with sharp eyes. All were watching for two small boys in a boat on a stormy sea.

But this was not all. The new motor life-boat was launched into the raging sea to take part in the search.

You can imagine how anxiously Tim's

father and mother waited all that night for news, and how tired and sad they were when the dawn came and still the boys had not been found.

For Tim and Ginger it was a bad dawn too. They peered over the side of the boat. Ahead of them was the land and at the water's edge a line of pointed rocks. The rocks were white with foam as great waves dashed over them.

‘We are on a lee shore,’ said Tim. ‘Be prepared to land, but I don’t like the look of it.’

At that moment a great wave hurled them towards the shore and smashed the boat against the rocks.

Ginger made a great jump and landed on a rock. But Tim was caught by the wave and dragged back into the sea.

Now Ginger was often silly and often a

coward. This time, however, he was brave. Though he could not swim, he dashed into the water and dragged Tim on to the rock.

'Ginger, you have saved my life,' gasped

Tim. 'Now we must try and get to the shore, though it does look difficult.'

Here, all Ginger's courage failed him. He fell on his knees and refused to move.

'I can't, I can't,' he cried. 'I am sure

there are cannibals on shore.'

'Don't be silly,' answered Tim. 'We are not on a desert island. We have not drifted as far as all that. Oh do come along.' But Ginger still refused to move.

Tim was just about to leave Ginger and scramble on shore for help, when he heard shouts and saw a party of four children climbing over the rocks towards them. They were saved at last.

It was a hard climb over the rocks. The

children helped them at the difficult places and then led them to a house near by.

Of course, Ginger, who saw they were just ordinary children, was now no longer frightened.

Once in the house, the elder boy rang up the coast-guard station and told them the news.

The elder girl made a big jug of hot cocoa, while the younger boy lit a great big fire.

In the meantime the little girl hurried upstairs to fetch warm, dry clothes for Tim

and Ginger to change into.
Soon Tim and Ginger were sitting by the fire drinking cocoa and feeling warm and comfortable.

The little girl said, 'Our mummy and daddy are on the cliff looking for you. I am glad we found you first.'

They were all sitting round the fire while Tim told them of his adventures, when in came the owner of the boat. He rushed upon Tim, caught him by the collar, and said, 'Ha!

You are the thief that stole my boat, aren't you? And now it's all smashed up. Come with me to the police station. I will see that you go to prison.'

'Unhand the boy!' came a great voice from the door-way. It was the voice of the old boatman who had followed close behind.

'Let the lad tell his story before you call him a thief.'

So Tim had to tell his story all over again. When he had finished, the old boatman said, 'The boy is not a thief. He is a hero.'

All the children cheered and Ginger hardest of all.

The next people to arrive were Tim's father and mother and a policeman.

You can just imagine how Tim's father and mother hugged Tim and Ginger, thanked the children and shook hands with the old boatman.

Tim had to tell his story all over again for the third time, and the policeman wrote every word of it down in his note-book.

Ginger was scolded for being so careless about the tide, but was praised for saving Tim from the sea.

The only person who was not happy was the owner of the boat. He kept on saying, 'Who is going to pay for my boat?'

Ginger said, 'Oh poof! Who's interested in your silly old boat!' At which everybody laughed; even the policeman.